# The Class Play

by Robert Newell
illustrated by Melissa Sweet

**D.C. Heath and Company**
Lexington, Massachusetts   Toronto, Ontario

My class was putting on a play.
It was about Peter Rabbit.

"Who wants to be Peter?" Miss Pepper asked.
I did! Peter Rabbit got to hop all over the stage.
I wanted to do that.
But Tim Sills got to be Peter.

"Who wants to be the farmer?" Miss Pepper asked.
I did! The farmer got to chase Peter under a fence.
I really wanted to do that.
But Larry Finn got to be the farmer.

"Does anyone want to be the mother?"
asked Miss Pepper.
I did! The mother rabbit got to shake her finger
and tell Peter what to do. That would be fun.
But Keesha Jones got to be the mother rabbit.

Then Miss Pepper asked about Flopsy and Mopsy.
Flopsy and Mopsy had to sing a song.
I could do that.  I like to sing.
But Mary and Cary Robb got to be
Flopsy and Mopsy.

There was only one part left. The carrot.
The carrot didn't hop or run or yell or sing.
It just stood there.
"Who wants to be the carrot?" Miss Pepper asked.
**I didn't!**

"It's hard to be a carrot, you know,"
Miss Pepper said.
"Carrots can't wiggle.  Carrots can't scratch.
They have to stand very still.
Now who would like to try?"

No one wanted to be the carrot.
So Miss Pepper had to pick somebody.
Guess who she picked.

Me.

The day of the play came.
Peter hopped all over the stage.
Then his rabbit suit fell down.  Oops!
I'm glad I wasn't Peter.

The farmer chased Peter.
Then he tripped on the fence.  Oops!
I'm glad I wasn't the farmer.

Mother Rabbit started to talk to Peter.
Then she forgot what words to say next.
She started to cry.  Poor Keesha!
I'm really glad I wasn't the mother rabbit.

Flopsy and Mopsy sang a song.
Then they got the giggles and couldn't stop.
That was the end of Flopsy and Mopsy.

Then I was all alone on the stage.
I didn't know what to do.
A carrot doesn't wiggle.  A carrot doesn't scratch.
I stood very still for a long, long time.
Then I took a bow.

Everybody clapped.
I think I was the star of the show!